The Great Pumpkin Strikes Again!

Based on the comic strips by Charles M. Schulz
Adapted by Justine and Ron Fontes
Art adapted by Tom Brannon

LITTLE SIMON
An imprint of Simon & Schuster Children's Publishing Division
New York   London   Toronto   Sydney
1230 Avenue of the Americas, New York, New York 10020
Manufactured in the United States of America
ISBN 0-689-87339-5
First Edition
2 4 6 8 10 9 7 5 3 1

Every Halloween, Linus waited in the pumpkin patch for the Great Pumpkin to appear. Every year he waited all night, hoping with all his might to catch a glimpse of his hero.

This year Peppermint Patty decided to give Linus a chance. "Okay, Linus, tell me all about the Great Pumpkin," she said.

"On Halloween night, the Great Pumpkin chooses the pumpkin patch that he thinks is the most sincere," Linus explained. "Then he rises out of the pumpkin patch and flies through the air bringing presents to children everywhere!"

"I believe you!" Peppermint Patty said excitedly. "I'm very superstitious, and the more impossible something is, the more I believe it. This Great Pumpkin story is impossible and ridiculous, but I believe it!"

Linus was amazed. Nobody ever listened to him about the Great Pumpkin.

After talking to Linus, Peppermint Patty headed over to the pumpkin patch to try his theory out—even though it was still a few days before Halloween. Her friend Marcie found her sitting in the middle of a big batch of orange pumpkins.

"Do you really believe in the Great Pumpkin, Sir?" Marcie asked.
Peppermint Patty shrugged. "I have to believe it, Marcie. I'm badly in need of a new baseball glove, and there are two whole months left until Christmas."

Linus was thrilled that someone else finally shared his belief in the Great Pumpkin. This year would be different! But having Peppermint Patty on his side wasn't enough. He needed to convince the others.

"If there's a Great Pumpkin, how come nobody has ever seen him?" his sister, Lucy, asked. "Answer me that!"

"You have very nice eyes, but you are completely out of your mind," Sally told her Sweet Babboo.

Even Snoopy didn't want to be recognized
waiting in the pumpkin patch with Linus.

Charlie Brown also didn't believe Linus. But when Linus wanted to write a letter to the Great Pumpkin, Charlie Brown agreed to help.

"All right, so we write a letter to the Great Pumpkin," Charlie Brown began. "Where do we send it?"

"To the Great Pumpkin in care of The Pumpkin Patch," replied Linus. "Where else?"

Charlie Brown looked at his friend and shook his head. "Where else, indeed," he said, and sighed. He just hoped Linus wouldn't be disappointed again.

There was only one day left before Halloween! The two true believers camped out in the pumpkin patch and began the long wait for their hero. Linus tingled with happy anticipation. He was sure this was the most sincere patch of all.

"Tomorrow is Halloween," he said happily.

Peppermint Patty was thrilled too. "Tomorrow I get my baseball glove," she exclaimed.

"Your what?!" Linus asked.

"My baseball glove," Peppermint Patty replied. "I asked the Great Pumpkin to bring me a new glove."

Linus could not believe his ears. "You don't ASK the Great Pumpkin for a present!" he shouted. "You wait for whatever he brings you! What do you think he is? Some kind of Santa Claus? Don't you know how sensitive he is? You've done the worst thing a person can do! You've offended the Great Pumpkin!"

Peppermint Patty covered her face in shame. All she wanted was a new baseball glove. She hadn't meant to hurt anybody's feelings. But perhaps believing in the Great Pumpkin was not the best way to acquire athletic equipment. She sadly walked away and sighed. "Banished from the pumpkin patch!"

So once again, on Halloween night, Linus sat in the pumpkin patch alone, waiting and hoping while the other kids paraded from house to house trick-or-treating.

As always, Lucy collected extra treats for her brother. With each house, she became more annoyed. *Why can't Linus just put on a costume and collect his own treats like everyone else?* she wondered. *It's bad enough that he has to ruin his own Halloween, but what about mine?*

The next morning Charlie Brown shook Linus awake. He'd come to tell his friend the big news.

"It was just on the radio," Charlie Brown said. "The Great Pumpkin appeared in a very sincere pumpkin patch owned by someone named Freeman in New Jersey."

Linus was cold and confused. He had fallen asleep in the pumpkin patch, another Halloween had come and gone, and the Great Pumpkin had not visited him.

Even though Linus was disappointed, he knew that the Great Pumpkin would visit again next Halloween. Linus was sure of it.

"Good-bye till next year, Great Pumpkin!" Linus said with hope in his heart—and, thanks to Lucy, trick-or-treat candy at home.